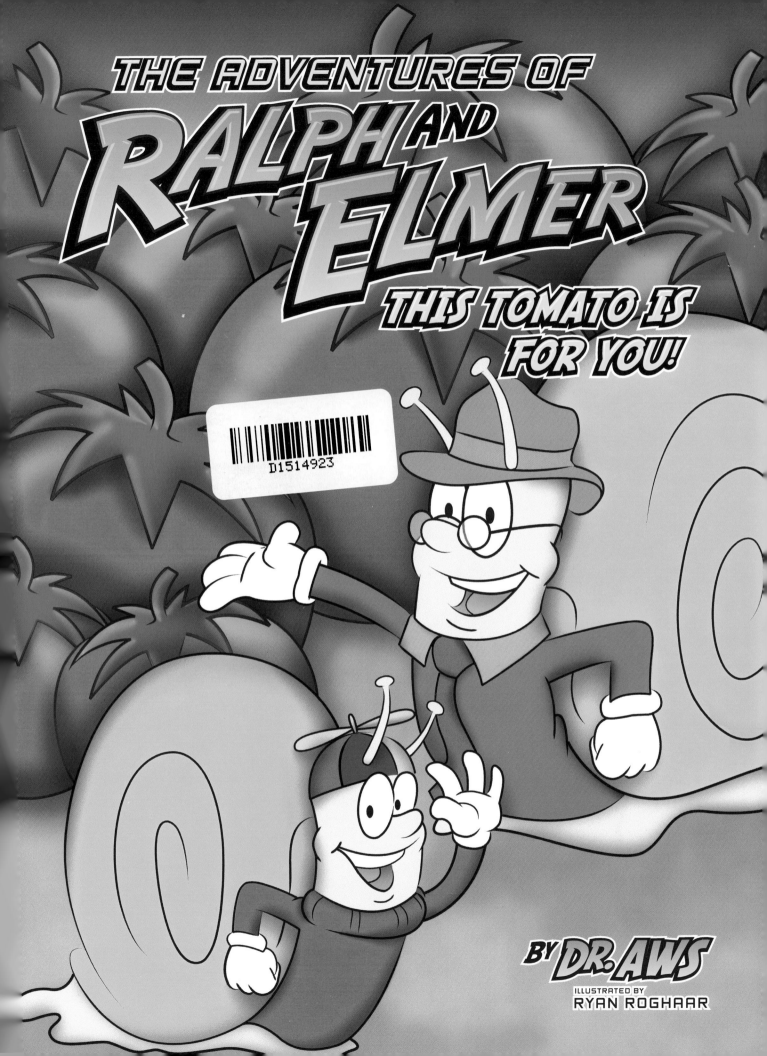

THE ADVENTURES OF RALPH AND ELMER: THIS TOMATO IS FOR YOU!

Published By:

Andromeda Press
Idaho

Book design, layout,
digital art, illustrations & cover: Ryan Roghaar

ISBN 978-0-9820649-0-0

DEDICATION

*T*hanking Jane, my wife, somehow seems inadequate as *The Adventures of Ralph and Elmer* finally reached fruition. She has listened to the numerous adventures of Ralph and Elmer, forever; wondering if I would write down these adventures for others to read. Jane has always encouraged me to complete *The Adventures of Ralph and Elmer,* so, here it is … and it's just for YOU.

Telling children about fruits and vegetables may seem unimportant to some, but what we eat, where it comes from, and connections to other world cultures can provide an understanding that all humans live in the same house… Earth.

While my imagination for the stories of Ralph and Elmer had few limitations, my talent as an artist did. I interviewed more than 40 artists and while they all were very talented, none captured the essence or spirit of Ralph and Elmer that I wanted to convey to children. A colleague of mine at the university, Brian Wells, was the first to capture the adventurousness of Ralph and Elmer and created the original illustrations for the first few pages. Brian's academic efforts consumed more and more of his time. As a result, he suggested a student, Ryan Roghaar. Ryan, as you will notice from every page of this book, is a great illustrator and has an imagination as crazy as mine; thus, we make a good team.

My sincerest thanks to Brian and his son, Donovan, for initially getting *The Adventures of Ralph and Elmer* from my brain to the printed page, to Ryan for his continued vision, and to Jane for her unwavering encouragement.

Inside the Professor's warm greenhouse lives a wise old snail named Ralph. Ralph helps the Professor grow many different plants. This time of year the Professor and Ralph are growing tomato plants.

Fred, the mail carrier, is bringing an envelope to Ralph.

"Hi, Fred," shouts Ralph. Ralph is expecting a letter from his grandson, Elmer.

"You have mail!" shouts Fred, waving the letter in the air.

Very excited about receiving mail, Ralph quickly opens the letter.
"WOW! My grandson, Elmer, is coming to visit today!" he
exclaims.

Ralph has cleaned his house and prepared Elmer's room.
Now he is sweeping the entrance to his beautiful home.

"It's going to be a lovely warm day in the greenhouse," thought Ralph
as he looked through the glass panes at the clear, blue morning sky.

Elmer arrives at the greenhouse. Excited about his arrival to his Grandpa's house, Elmer takes a deep breath and says in a low whisper, "Wow! This is a wonderful place."

Elmer enters the door carrying his two suitcases and begins to look for his Grandpa's home.

"Grandpa… Grandpa Ralph, I am here!" shouted Elmer as loud as his voice would let him.

"Elmer… Where are you?" said Ralph as he looked over the table's ledge where his home was located.

"Down here, Grandpa!" said Elmer.

"Elmer!" Ralph exclaimed as he looked down to see Elmer near the greenhouse doorway.

"Good morning, Grandpa Ralph," said Elmer, "How do I get up to you?"

"Good morning, Elmer. You can use the ramp to your left."

"Elmer, it's been two years since our last visit."

"It's good to see you again Grandpa," replied Elmer as he stared at all the plants and the large red things hanging from the stems. "What are those?" asked Elmer, pointing. "Those are tomatoes," answered Ralph.

"What is a tomato? Is it a vegetable, Grandpa?" asked a puzzled Elmer. "Well, actually, Elmer, a tomato is a fruit."

"Wow, really?" Elmer was amazed.

"Indeed, it is a fruit, and it is full of vitamin C. Vitamin C is very important. It will help you to grow up big and strong. And, tomatoes are very tasty, too!" continued Grandpa Ralph.

Ralph took Elmer over to a green tomato that was near his home. "This tomato is not ripe. When it is ripe it will turn into a red delicious tomato."

"You sure know a lot about tomatoes," Grandpa Ralph. "How do you know so much about plants?"

"The Professor and I have studied plants for many years. I have lived here in the greenhouse with the Professor since I was just a little snail about your age."

"Who is the Professor?" asked Elmer.

"He is the very smart man who owns the greenhouse, and he speaks fluent Snail," answered Ralph.

Elmer listened to his grandfather's words, especially the ones about tomatoes making you healthy and strong. Elmer thought, "If I eat more tomatoes and drink more tomato juice, I could be the strongest snail in the world!"

Elmer's daydream was interrupted by his grandfather's voice.

"Elmer… Elmer! What are you thinking about?"

"Oh, Grandpa, I am thinking about how tomatoes make you strong."

"Yes, Elmer, tomatoes contain a lot of vitamin A and vitamin C. They help young boys and girls grow into healthy and strong adults. The Professor told me the tomato was once called the Apple of Paradise, and sometimes it is even known as the Peru Apple," Ralph said as he moved toward his home.

Ralph gave Elmer a straw to try some tomato juice.

Elmer stuck the straw into the tomato as his Grandpa continued to talk. Soon Elmer was sipping tomato juice through his straw.

After several large sips of tomato juice, Elmer stopped and shouted, "Wow, Grandpa, fresh tomato juice, it sure tastes like paradise!"

Elmer's drink of tomato juice is suddenly interrupted. Rain drops fall on Elmer's Head. This is strange. "Wait, rain in a greenhouse? This can not be!" thinks a puzzled Elmer. "Why is there so much water? Where is it coming from? Is this a daydream?"

Soon the entire table is filled with water. The water begins to push Elmer over the table's edge. "This is not a dream!" thinks Elmer.

Ralph notices the water, too. He is afraid. He had not been afraid for a long time. His mouth opens wide to warn Elmer, but no words come out!

Elmer thought this was the end. What a sad ending to be washed away. Elmer tries to yell for help, but no sound comes out.

Ralph is panicked. "What about Elmer?" He is being carried faster and faster toward the drain. "What will happen if my grandson is washed down the drain?"

Just as Elmer is being pushed ever closer to the greenhouse drain, Ralph sees the Professor in the doorway.

Elmer finds his voice and screams, "STOP!" His voice is so loud the greenhouse windows rattle. The Professor, startled by the loud voice, releases the handle on the hose nozzle. The water flow was shut off. "Who screamed stop?" asks the Professor.

A tiny voice says, "Down here." The Professor looks toward the drain. He is surprised to see a small snail looking up at him. Elmer says again, "Down here!"

"Are you the tiny one with such a loud voice?" asked the Professor. "Yes. My name is Elmer. My grandfather, Ralph lives in the green-house and I am visiting him."

The Professor turns to Ralph who is still on the table. "How long has he been here?"

"He just arrived today. I was telling him how I've enjoyed hearing you talk about vegetables and fruits."

The Professor and Ralph nearly forgot about Elmer. A tiny voice comes from the floor. "Down here, Grandpa, down here!" There is Elmer, hanging on the Professor's shoelace to keep from falling farther into the drain.

The Professor reaches his hand down. "Elmer, let me help you back to the tabletop," the Professor says as he cradles Elmer in his hand.

Ralph thanks the Professor for his kindness in saving Elmer.

"Ralph, I am very glad to meet your grandson. I hope we can visit often when I'm here in the greenhouse," the Professor said.

Ralph smiles with the thought of talking to the Professor about his plants. "Elmer will learn so much, too!" he tells the Professor.

The Professor reaches out and picks a big tomato from a tall bush. "Here, Elmer. This Tomato is for YOU," whispers the professor.

"Wow! My very own tomato!" shouts Elmer as he beams with pride.

"Professor, I was telling Elmer about tomatoes and how they provide many vitamins for people and snails."

"They do provide many vitamins. Do you know the tomato was once called the Peru Apple?"

"Yes, my Grandpa told me you said that. But, why were they called the Peru Apple?" asks Elmer.

"Because, more than a thousand years ago all tomatoes came from Peru in South America," the Professor replied.

"But, how did the tomatoes get to Europe and then to America?" Elmer asks.

"Wait a minute, and I will show you!" shouts the Professor as he disappeared from the greenhouse.

"Where did he go, Grandpa?" asks a concerned Elmer.

"Oh, he'll be back. He's a teacher, and this is one of those teachable moments!"

Soon the Professor returns carrying a tiny computer.

The Professor places the computer on the tabletop, and Elmer begins striking keys. Soon a map of South America appears on the screen.

The Professor glances at the tiny computer. "Wow, Elmer, you have already found Peru!"

Elmer beams with pride, "Yes! I used to watch the man where I lived before work on his computer every night."

The Professor tells Ralph and Elmer about the history of the tomato. "The Indian tribes of Peru carried the tomato fruit and seeds to Central America. The Aztecs grew tomatoes in Mexico and offered them to Cortez about the year 1519 as a gift from one of their Gods, Quetzalcoatl. The Spanish took the tomatoes and seeds back to Spain where the tomatoes were carried to other countries of the world."

"Wow!" shouts Elmer. "That was great. Can you tell us more, Professor, please!" pleads Elmer.

Ralph and Elmer are glad the professor is taking the time to teach them about the history of tomatoes.

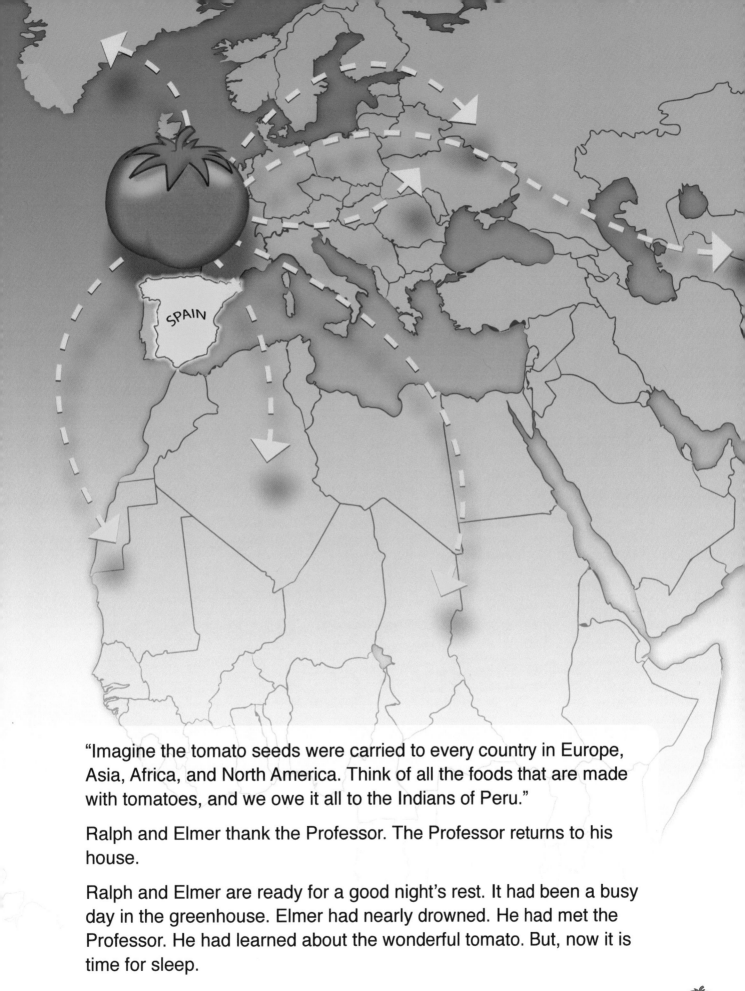

"Imagine the tomato seeds were carried to every country in Europe, Asia, Africa, and North America. Think of all the foods that are made with tomatoes, and we owe it all to the Indians of Peru."

Ralph and Elmer thank the Professor. The Professor returns to his house.

Ralph and Elmer are ready for a good night's rest. It had been a busy day in the greenhouse. Elmer had nearly drowned. He had met the Professor. He had learned about the wonderful tomato. But, now it is time for sleep.

Ralph guides Elmer to his house. When they go to Elmer's room, Elmer says with a sleepy yawn, "Will you read me a bedtime story?"

Ralph thinks, "What story shall I read?" He thinks even harder; then, it comes to him. He reaches for an old brown book on the bookshelf. His great-great-grandfather's journal of his adventures along the Oregon Trail would be perfect!

He begins to read to Elmer. "The morning sun had not yet risen. The fog hugged the water's edge. All the wagons were arranged to start westward. It was a new beginning for our small snail family. We were about to leave St. Louis for a new home in the West. What would we find?"

After many weeks on the Oregon Trail, the wagon train carrying Jonathan Driggs and his wife Martha arrived at Independence Rock, the last stop before entering the Northwest Territory. The wagon train was nearly a mile long, and Jonathan and Martha were in the very last wagon. They climbed on the edge of the wagon's rear gate and looked at all the tracks left by the parade of their wagons.

Jonathan wrote in his journal, "We were the only snails on the wagon train. We were so alone, leaving all our friends and family back in Georgia."

Jonathan had more to write. "Martha and I have found our new home, not by choice but by the strangest of accidents. The wagon train was near Fort Hall. Martha and I slipped into a bucket hanging from the rear of the wagon to take a bath in the cool water. Suddenly, the wagon hit a huge rock. The bucket flew off the wagon's rear gate, tumbling down a hill. We held on to each other as the bucket rolled and rolled, spilling most of the water. When it finally stopped and we peered out, the wagon train was only a distant spot moving west. We were in a new strange land. This was our home now, and we would have to make the best of it."

Ralph sees that Elmer is fast asleep. He marks the page in the journal and goes to sleep, too.

Elmer dreams that night of all the wonderful adventures that he, his Grandpa, and the Professor will soon have…

THE ADVENTURES OF RALPH AND ELMER
THIS TOMATO IS FOR YOU!

The Adventures of Ralph and Elmer: This Tomato is for You! is the first in a series of books designed to provide accurate information for elementary school aged children regarding the origin of various fruits, herbs, and vegetables. To extend the learning possibilities and encourage interactive projects, a greenhouse growing kit for each featured vegetable and fruit in the specific book is available.

All supplemental materials can be acquired through the Ralph and Elmer website (www.ralphandelmer.com)

The Adventures of Ralph and Elmer: Miniature Greenhouse

Just like the professor, students can use this Mini-greenhouse to grow their very own crop of the vegetable featured in the story. With illustrated instructions for sowing the seed, tending the plant, transplanting, and harvesting kids will see sprouts in no time!

Kit includes seeds, soil, pots, and miniature greenhouse.

The Adventures of Ralph and Elmer: Interactive CD-ROM

This interactive CD-ROM (for both Mac and PC) will give young readers the opportunity to continue the adventure they began in the book by following Ralph and Elmer on their escapades in the greenhouse and beyond!

The Ralph and Elmer: Cookbook

Delicious tomato recipes with step-by-step instructions and accompanying illustrations to aid in preparing the tomato dishes for the entire family. Many of the recipes will be from different regions of the world and will be highlighted by a brief story of their origin in the culture of that country.

The Ralph and Elmer: Science Activity Book

Each tomato science booklet will be grade specific, pre-school to fourth grade. The hands-on science activities will foster the development of basic science process skills such as observing, measuring, classifying, using numbers, inferring, predicting communicating, and formulating hypotheses.

ORDER ONLINE AT WWW.RALPHANDELMER.COM